DATE DUE

FEB 2 0 1997		
AUG 1 2 1997		
JAN 0 2 1998		
JAN 3 0 1998		
JAN 3 2000		
MAR 1 5 2000		
APR 2 4 2001		
JUL 2 9 2002		
AUG 1 1 2015		

ROBIN HOOD

Retold & illustrated by

CAROL HEYER

Ideals Children's Books • Nashville, Tennessee

Published by Ideals Publishing Corporation
Nashville, Tennessee 37214

Printed and bound in the United States of America.

Library of Congress Cataloging-in-Publication Data
Heyer, Carol, 1950-
Robin Hood / retold and illustrated by Carol Heyer.
    p.   cm.
Summary: Recounts the life and adventures of Robin Hood, who, with his band of
followers, lived in Sherwood Forest as an outlaw dedicated to fighting tyranny.
ISBN 0-8249-8634-2 (trade)
ISBN 0-8249-8648-2 (lib. bdg.)
1. Robin Hood (Legendary character)—Juvenile literature. [1. Robin Hood
(Legendary character)
2. Folklore—England] I. Robin Hood (Legend). English. II. Title.
PZ8.1.H487Ro 1993
398.22 – dc20
[E]   93-18591
                                                                 CIP
                                                                    AC

As always this book is dedicated to my parents, William J. Heyer and Merlyn
Hutson Heyer. Also for my Aunt Ailsa Hutson and my friends Frances, Ernie,
Julia, Monica, and Andrea Ruiz.   —C.H.

I would like to thank my family and friends who so graciously gave of their time to
help me with this project.   —C.H.

Characters	
Robin in the Hood	Anthony Leko
Sir Richard o' the Lea	Ronald Clyburn
Friar Tuck	William J. Heyer
King Richard	Richard Hallack
Will Scarlett	Bill Mahoney
Adam o' the Dell	David Atkinson
Much the Miller's Son	Devin Carter
Dick O'Banbury	Dwayne Carter

The illustrations in this book were rendered in pencils and acrylics using live models.
The text type is set in Berkeley Book.
The display type is set in Caslon Openface with Goudy Text Lombardic Initial Caps.
Color separations were made by Rayson Films, Inc., Waukesha, Wisconsin.
Printed and bound by Worzalla Publishing, Stevens Point, Wisconsin.

Designed by Joy Chu.

First Edition
10 9 8 7 6 5 4 3 2 1

In a long ago and faraway time, unhappiness engulfed the people of England. The poor and hungry commoners of this land lived in great fear of their ruthless leaders. One such leader was the Sheriff of Nottingham, who took from the rich and the poor alike, punishing anyone unwilling to pay his demands.

Only one individual in all the realm stood willingly against the evil Sheriff—the outlaw "Robin in the Hood." Storytellers whispered that Robin had once been falsely accused of stealing the King's deer, a crime punishable by death. Fearing for his life, the young man had fled to the safety of Sherwood Forest, where he hid among the trees wearing a hooded suit of Lincoln green.

Helped by fellow fugitives, known as his band of Merry Men, Robin Hood imposed his own brand of justice upon a dark and lawless land. He soon became a champion of the people by taking from the rich to give to the poor . . .

Robin and his men enjoyed their favorite pastime of waylaying a traveler with whom to share their evening feast. At the dinner table, Robin always asked for payment. If the diner lied about how much money he had, then the Merry Men took all of his money for the poor. But if the traveler was honest, he was simply allowed to go along his way.

One quiet summer day, Robin Hood sent Little John, Will Scarlett, and Much the Miller's Son in search of a dinner guest. The late afternoon sun followed the band of Merry Men, and soon they heard the whinny of an approaching horse. The outlaws spread across the road and blocked the way of a poorly dressed knight as he plodded toward them.

Taking the reins, Little John said, "Sir Knight, my master, Robin Hood, has bade me to bring you to our feast this summer's evening beneath the Great Oak in Sherwood."

The knight replied, "I have heard of your good master and would gladly accept his invitation, but I am not good company this night."

Little John persisted. Soon the knight agreed, but he fell silent, and his features darkened with sadness as he followed the men to camp.

Upon their arrival at the Great Oak, Robin dropped to the ground before them and said, "I am your host, Robin Hood. Welcome to our table."

"I am Sir Richard of the Lea," the knight responded, "and I thank you for your hospitality to me, a poor knight."

Robin smiled and said, "Ah, but Sir Knight, I have never found one of your station to be poor. I tell you now that in order to set this splendid table, we must charge our guests a fee."

The knight softly said, "I have but ten shillings in my purse."

Robin laughed, saying, "Then give your purse to Little John, and if he finds no more than that, I will not take a penny of it from you."

Little John spread the contents of the purse on his cloak and counted it. There he found ten shillings, as the knight had said—no more, no less.

"What trouble has befallen you, Sir Knight?" Robin inquired.

"My son accidentally killed another knight in a jousting match," Sir Richard replied. "The Sheriff of Nottingham wrongly held him for ransom."

Robin and his men listened as Sir Richard explained that he had sold his goods and mortgaged his estate for four hundred pounds to Prior Vincent of St. Mary's. While the money had freed Sir Richard's son, the greedy Prior Vincent had given the knight very little time to pay him back.

"And now," the knight sadly finished, "It is time for repayment. I am on my way to St. Mary's Priory to sign over my lands."

Robin jumped to his feet and shouted, "I know of that wretched Prior Vincent. We will not allow him to steal yet another man's land!"

He turned to his men and said, "Little John, fetch four hundred pounds from the coffers for Sir Richard. And you shall accompany him to St. Mary's as his guard and squire."

Overcome with happiness, Sir Richard vowed on his sword to return to this same spot, one year to the day, to repay his debt.

As Sir Richard and Little John rode into St. Mary's, Prior Vincent sat at a great table spread with platters piled high with food. On his left sat the Sheriff of Nottingham to protect him. On his right sat the High Cellarer to bear witness to the proceedings.

The sound of horses' hooves caused the men to glance at one another anxiously. They watched as Sir Richard entered the chamber alone. As a true test of the Prior's heart, the knight sought to make them think that he had no money to repay his loan. He knelt before the three men sadly.

"Did you bring the money to ransom your lands?" the Prior's voice chirped fretfully.

"Not a penny do I have, but come instead to seek mercy and request more time to repay my debt."

The Prior smiled broadly at the High Cellarer, rubbing his hands together greedily. His voice boomed out, "Bear witness to this Knight's default and mark that his lands are now mine."

No sooner had those words left the Prior's lips than the knight jumped to his feet.

"You are no true Churchman," Sir Richard shouted, "for you have no charity in your heart."

At that moment, Little John stamped in and slammed a chest on the already full table. Prior Vincent stared at the chest as Little John threw the lid back to reveal the money. The Prior's expression changed from smugness to anger as he realized that he had lost.

Autumn, winter, and spring passed in Sherwood in much the same manner, as guests were invited to dine with the outlaws and then were relieved of their excess money. On one of these days, Little John, Will, and Much dropped from the trees to waylay a cloaked Churchman heading down the Londontown Road.

This Churchman fell in behind the two, clutching his cloak tightly about him and praying that no one would recognize him. Not until they reached the trysting tree did Little John notice that their guest happened to be the High Cellarer of St. Mary's. Little John swung up into the tree to reveal this identity to Robin.

When Robin and Little John joined the group, Robin circled the Cellarer and spoke tauntingly, "Methinks I recognize this monk!" Then he turned to Little John and winked. "What say you, Little John? Could this be the High Cellarer of St. Mary's who stood against our good Sir Richard?" Little John rubbed his chin and squinted his eyes at the Churchman.

"Ay, Robin," Little John answered, "you are right. It is indeed the selfsame man that stood against us."

"How much money do you carry to Londontown?" Robin asked roughly, pulling at the Churchman's cloak.

"Sir Robin," the Cellarer said nervously, "I fear you have mistaken me for some other. I know nothing of this Richard. I am on a holy pilgrimage and have but twenty marks upon me. I beg you to let me continue on my prayerful path."

Robin gestured for Little John to search the Churchman's horse. In the saddlebags, Little John found not twenty marks, but eight hundred pounds! The Merry Men dumped the coins into their own coffers and sent the empty-handed monk on his way. Robin Hood and his men then celebrated, for the money taken from Sir Richard had been repaid twofold.

Soon the day arrived when Sir Richard returned to the Great Oak. Bringing his packhorses to a halt, he dismounted and opened a small chest on the back of a horse. Four hundred or more gold coins sparkled brightly in the afternoon sun.

Then Sir Richard unwrapped bundles of the finest bows the men had ever seen. Carved of rich wood, hand polished, and inlaid with the finest silver threads, each bow came with a quiver of silver-tipped arrows. The knight handed Robin Hood a bow wrought with gold and an ornate quiver filled with gold-tipped arrows.

Robin and his men cheered for these fine weapons, but the coins they returned. When Sir Richard insisted that they keep the money, Robin quickly explained that the High Cellarer of St. Mary's had supped with them this week past and had found it in his heart to repay Sir Richard's debt twofold.

During their evening feast, Sir Richard warned Robin of an archery contest soon to be held. The greatest bowmen would compete for a golden arrow offered by the Sheriff of Nottingham. Since the Sheriff was more in the habit of taking gold than giving it, Sir Richard reasoned that the contest must surely be a trap for Robin Hood.

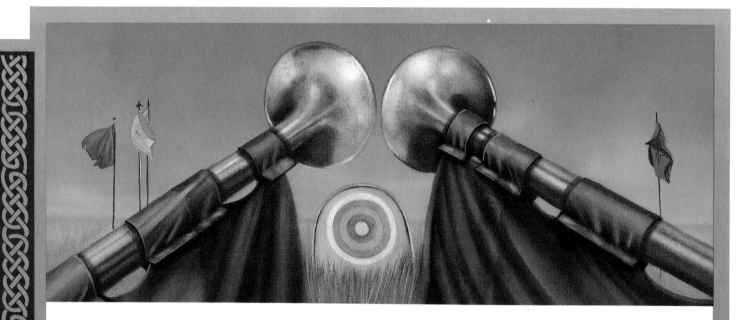

The day of the shooting match soon came. Brilliant flags waved above the pavilions that sheltered tables of food. Targets were placed on the open field. On one side, in a roped-off area, stood the common folk, and on a raised and covered platform sat the nobles. The Sheriff, his Lady, and Prior Vincent each had an eye out for Robin Hood. Men-at-arms circled the camp, seeking the same quarry.

The archers were called to begin the competition. To the front limped a stranger dressed all in scarlet, with his hair tucked beneath a wide-brimmed hat. Across one eye he wore a leather patch.

With each round, the stranger's arrows struck the center of the target until there remained but two finalists—Adam o' the Dell and the stranger. The last target was placed, and Adam o' the Dell came forward to shoot. His arrow hit dead on center. The crowd cheered.

Slowly limping forward, the stranger carefully chose his arrow. Then he nocked it, raised his bow, and fired, all in one swift movement. To the astonishment of all, the stranger's arrow flew true, splitting Adam o' the Dell's cleanly down the center. The crowd's roar was deafening. Never had anyone seen such a magnificent shot.

The stranger limped to the platform, where the Sheriff's Ladywife awarded him the golden arrow.

"Never in my life have I seen marksmanship such as yours," cried the Sheriff, clapping the stranger on the back. "You have fairly won the golden arrow this day, for you are without doubt the best archer in all these lands!"

Grandly the stranger waved his arm and bowed to the Sheriff in a mocking gesture.

"Master archer," the Sheriff whined, "will you honor me and join my service? I would be happy to have someone as skilled as you in my ranks."

The stranger stiffened.

"I will not join your service," his sharp voice rang out in a familiar tone. "I am my own man, and no one in all of England shall be my master."

With that, the stranger pulled the hat from his head, ripped the patch from his eye, and threw the scarlet cloak from his shoulders. The crowd gasped as they realized that it was Robin of the Hood.

A cheer went up and many of the poorer folk stood in the way of the soldiers as they rushed at Robin. In the chaos, Robin took his prize, mounted his horse, and raced with his men from Nottingham without firing an arrow.

The enraged Sheriff gathered his soldiers and gave chase. They followed the bandits far into Sherwood Forest, deep in the heart of the outlaws' domain.

Suddenly outlaws began to appear from nowhere, dropping from the

trees and surrounding the Sheriff and his men. When the Sheriff realized their uneven odds, he turned and ran. Though his horse moved quickly, he could not escape an arrow loosed by Little John. It would be well over a month before the Sheriff could sit comfortably again.

The Sheriff's suffering at the hands of Robin Hood had become too great for him to bear. Once his wound had healed, the Sheriff of Nottingham took his grievances to the King.

"Your majesty, I need your help," the Sheriff pleaded. "I need royal soldiers and an edict from the King. I am begging Your Highness to help me." The King listened carefully to the Sheriff's charges, and then he called in one of his knights, Sir Richard's own son Henry.

"Sir Henry," the King began, "you are from the part of the county where Robin Hood and his men live. I would give a purse of gold if I could meet with this Robin in the Hood."

"My father knows him well," Sir Henry replied. "If Your Majesty is indeed willing to lose a purse of gold, I know of a way that you can not only meet with Robin Hood, but feast with him and his men in Sherwood."

"How would you bring this about?" asked the King.

"If you put on the robes of the Order of Black Friars and hang a purse filled with golden coins at your waist, all that is left is to ride through Sherwood Forest. Robin Hood will see to the rest."

"Then tomorrow we shall ride!" laughed the King.

The next morning, the Sheriff went on his way to Nottingham as a small group of Black Friars rode slowly into the shadows of Sherwood. Soon Robin himself stepped out onto the road in front of them.

"Methinks I see a fat purse dangling at your side, good Friar," Robin said, eyeing the monk carefully. "And I am sure that you could gladly give a portion of that to those less fortunate than yourself."

The King replied, "While it is true that I have forty pounds in my purse, I see no reason to give the money of the church so freely to you."

"Forty pounds is a great sum," Robin replied. "And if that is all you carry, we shall keep but half of it—and not for ourselves, but for the poor."

Little John took the purse from the King. He spread the coins on his mantle and counted. Finding exactly forty pounds, he kept half and returned the rest to the King. Then Robin led the friars to the ancient Oak in Sherwood, where they ate and drank and had a merry time.

"At our monastery, we have heard great tales of your skill," the King said after dinner, "and that of your men, with the longbow. I would very much like to see a sampling of those skills."

Robin ordered a garland of flowers to be set up on one end of the glade. Each man would shoot three arrows through the center of the flowers. If any man missed, he would receive a buffet from Will Scarlett's fist.

Little John shot first, and all three arrows hit their mark. Then Much the Miller's Son fired. His first two arrows scored, but his third missed. Everyone laughed as he went to stand in front of Will Scarlett, ready to receive his punishment.

Will slapped his hand against the loser's chin, knocking him down. Much sat on the ground, rubbed his sore jaw, and rolled his eyes to heaven, while the men broke into laughter. The King himself laughed till the tears ran down his face.

Thus it went for the entire afternoon. Each man took his turn; some hit their marks while others stepped forward to receive their strike.

Finally Robin Hood's turn came. His first arrow struck the very center of the garland. His second arrow clipped the tip of the first, and, as usual, all wondered at his skill.

Then Robin let fly the third arrow. Unfortunately it was ill-feathered and landed outside the garland.

"Foul!" he cried. "I knew that feather was wrong as the shaft left my fingers." His men had never seen him miss a shot before, but they would not let him escape his slap.

"Then I will only take my punishment from this holy friar; a tap from him will be my penance." He turned to the King. "Will you deal my punishment with your holy hands?" The King's men smiled at one another, stepping back in anticipation.

"Gladly," said the King. "It will help make up for the twenty pounds you took from my purse."

"If you can knock me to the ground, good Friar, then I will cheerfully return your money," smiled Robin. "But if you cannot, then I will take every penny that you have left."

The King stepped forward and rolled back his sleeve. He swung back and slammed Robin with a blow like a thunderbolt. Robin Hood dropped to the ground while his men began to howl with laughter, for the holy friar hit far harder than Will Scarlett would have struck his own leader. Slowly Robin got to his feet and reluctantly handed the King back his twenty pounds.

Suddenly they heard the sound of hoofbeats and shouting as Sir Richard of the Lea galloped into their midst.

"Robin," he cried. "I come to warn you that the King is out now looking for you. You and your men must come with me to my castle at Briarlea and hide there till the danger is past."

As Sir Richard jumped from his mount, his eyes locked with those of the King, whom he recognized at once. He flung himself upon his knees in front of the supposed friar.

When the King saw that Sir Richard recognized him, he threw back the black robe to reveal his royal crest. All knelt before him.

But the King's eyes returned to Sir Richard as he asked, "How dare you offer these men refuge in your castle, knowing that I sought them?"

"I could not let harm come to them," Sir Richard answered, "for I owe Robin Hood my life, my honor . . . everything."

"Rise, all of you," said the King, whose frown was melting into a smile, "for none will be harmed by me this day.

"Robin Hood, I hereby give you and all of your men free pardon. From this day forward, you shall live with me in Londontown."

Early the next morning, each man rode in the train of the King, with Robin in the Hood at his right hand.

obin Hood and his Merry Men lived for many years in the King's service. Though they had left their forest home, they never gave up fighting for the common people, helping the poor, and assisting the downtrodden.

After many years had passed, the silent call of the greenwood grew so strong that Robin Hood could no longer resist it. He and his men returned to the forest of Sherwood, where they lived till the end of their days.